PLEASURABLE ENCOUNTERS-
Black Velvet

To order additional copies of this book, contact:
Xlibris
844-714-8691
www.Xlibris.com
Orders@Xlibris.com

ISBN: Softcover   978-1-6641-9036-8
         EBook   978-1-6641-9035-1

Print information available on the last page

Rev. date: 08/18/2021

PLEASURABLE ENCOUNTERS-
Black Velvet

JUSTINA LIGHT

PLEASURABLE ENCOUNTERS- BLACK VELVET

Black Velvet always wore black velvet gowns, she was an erotic type of an American African Woman, didn't reveal or expose too much of her womanly body parts or her sexy points of her body type's, which were very reserved by her.

Katherine always wondered if sex would be interesting with her. She loved how tall she was, about six feet tall, with very jet black blue hair, passed her back –with very long curly hair colour tone, along with her lovely skin tone- which was soft and beautiful, and shined like a radiant rare diamond.

Her African American weather climate-had given her a milky look of shade--a sexy appeal, to her entire body image skin-- giving it a sexy appearance—to her, to the naked eye—she was very attractive, woman. Katherine always wondered if they got together, in a sexual way-if sex would be wonderful and appealing to the extreme of excitement—for both of them, in fantasy roles, and role playing, was part of her imagination.

Katherine was approximately five point four inches, in height with light blonde and kinky curly hair, which made her look fun and energetic, and extremely sexy. She also had wide open eyes-like an almond nut shape-giving it a pointy look-- on her edges of her eyes-that seemed so sexy, looking like a leopard cat. Her bright blue eyes were radiant to look at and glare in them, and get lost in them as you stared in them— with deep desire-of lust.

Katherine was too shy to seduce anyone-even though she was extremely a sexy woman herself. She had two great pairs of legs, and a great figure to show off-she had many erotic sexual experiences with many erotic sexual women- many lesbians of females—that she had chosen, which she was attracted too. Her deep desire was to have an encounter with Black Velvet, and enter her world of fantasies, and lust-of temptations.

She would think, how wonderful it would be to have a chance to enhance her sexual needs with Black Velvet, and get to please her completely—in every way.

She was very hungry for Black Velvet, and all she thought was about Black Velvet's Pussy- which she had seen-many times-- her taking long showers in her shower tub, a while ago—as she would occasionally watch her take a shower, in their bathroom. She would wait for her to come out from the shower door and dry her sexy body off with these tender cloth towels, which turned her on completely, as she rubs each part of her body—in an erotic move as-- the encounters would begin—just after that.

Watching Black Velvet-get dress, was a big turn on for Katherine, and then they would go out for a bite to eat, which was hard to concentrate with all the excitement going on in the city, about how good she looked in the shower bare naked.

At times, she wanted to take her right- there sexually in the bathroom -having great sex with her, was what they lived for-while she gets out from the shower tub to the dry mat, and places her sexy toes on the mat-where she would dry herself up -- and make her stare without touching her—these were some of her games, played by her rules—always making her suffer—and teaching her to have patience for what she wanted, the most. All she was hoping to have was wild sex with Black Velvet, which she found her extremely sexy and really erotic, looking—and her games were something she liked and admired—it was all about control and power.

At times, she would glance at Black Velvet pussy, which was soaked and wet, from taking a shower.

Her pussy was completely shaven-except some light hairs on top of the crown of her cunt area and it was a big turn on for Katherine—to look at and wonder, how it would taste in her mouth-as she stares at it, with delight-as she also had a tattoo on her upper pelvic of a black cobra snake-as the snake had a large tongue sticking out from his mouth.

She loved how the artist drew the fangs of the Cobra-as it was dangerous and evil-that suited Black Velvet lifestyle. At times Black Velvet would slither away with her tongue –tasting Katherine –and also lightly nipping on her body-but didn't dare to bite her hard, and poison her-to the point of no return.

At times-she would bite her a bit harder -only if she was directed to- do so-as it would leave a small hickey, on her body-as the Cobra mouth had landed and had curse her in divine-temptation.

A couple strands of hairs would crown-Black Velvet top pussy - and giving it some character, displaying her sexuality from her vagina area-that it was her way of keeping it attractive looking-for Katherine. As, she was curse by Black Velvet-under her spell- as she knew that the curse was given by the king of Balaam-as the Cobra was Curse, itself-as a serpent that spend most of his life slithering on the ground—and not living in upper society, of norms.

At times, they watched porn's that were odd, in behaviour-in curses of snakes-and demons- as they enjoyed Satan lifestyles- according to their encounters-it was known to be forbidden, from the outside word. As, they both didn't live by Genesis orders- it happened that they like disobeying—as the concept of lifestyles had changed in society—as many couples would dramatize what they wanted in their lives-and not go according to older traditions-of lifestyles.

These cruse ceremonies were taken place often, by both of them—as they knew they were called curses of hell- as they both molded together-and answer to Balaam orders-as they shall enjoy their lyrics of life—as they had chosen-a lustful way of blessing life-from their own eyesight's-as they would flacked together- as they spoke to each other-with sweet voices-of what they wanted from each other-in performance.

At times Katherine, would think her pussy would display a sexy woman of character, which gives an impression that Black Velvet was open to many different types of encounters-and was free to a lifestyle of lust and desire's—and didn't have to follow the rules of these other harsh creatures on land, that didn't agree to these outer lifestyle of creations.

Black Velvet was proud of being a sexy African American Woman-and she loved showing off her sexy curvy hips, while coming out from the shower door-and rubbing cocoa butter on her entire body to moisten it up from any dryness that might be there, from before-and then she would concentrate at her curvy hips, that were luxurious, to add more cocoa butter to soften her dry areas, of her skin.

She looked extremely sexy, when taking a shower and rubbing her body with plenty of silky liquid soap from the bottle-with her silky sponge on her tender body, cleansing herself. At times, she would concentrate on her Cobra Snake tattoo-as she took the time to cleanse it.

Her silky wet kinky curly hair-would reached her lower back, which made her look so tempting to get fucked in the shower, by Katherine. Her Cobra snake made her look so daring-and so unique-as she loved a women who was very graphic in style.

Katherine knew that Black Velvet, always preferred to take showers on her own-and she didn't mind if Katherine would watch her take one alone, it would increase her self-esteem that she was desirable, and someone was interested in her, and watching her, from far.

At times, it was difficult for Katherine to resist-and she was hoping that Black Velvet would change her mind by allowing her to join her in the shower, with her. It rarely didn't happen, and Katherine needed to accept it, as part of her private time, being alone, with herself.

The shower sprinkler, would drip water down on Black Velvet face and on her hair and then her entire body, which was a sexy type of a touch to look at her entirely naked body getting wet, and it seemed like she was part of an art sculpture, so beautiful, in every detail-as she looked like an art piece, of collections.

The water drops would remain on her body from the water sprinkler fountain-and would slowly diminish away from each drop of water that would dropped on her beautiful skin - as it touched her wet moist body, it would run down on her bare legs and then to her soft toes, and then gradually disappearing.

At that point-Katherine wanted her so badly, she was the aggressive kind of a lover-and decides to seduce her first-by dominating her and seducing her, by being patience with her rules and deep wants.

Most of the time, Black Velvet would get closer to Katherine, while Katherine would sit on the coach- waiting for her, while she would finish taking her shower-and Black Velvet would grab Katherine's hands and place them on her sexy soaking cunt, by opening her legs wide open and placing her fingers on her bare clit, and asking her to rub it and suck it hard. She would enjoy how she would use her fingers-going all around her pussy area to enhance sexual desire and needs.

Then she begs her, to use her long tongue to enhance it and give it pleasure, with her wet touches of her tender tongue-towards her clit area- to excite her, more.

"Eat my cunt out" she begs Katherine, by saying to her- "I really want it badly from you- I want you to eat out my juicy cunt out, like a dirty slut-with your horny mouth-eat me up." Black Velvet begs Katherine to do as she says-and dirty talk to her-a she likes Profanity in her Sex Play.

"I want you to make me cum with your mouth, and Fuck my cunt out with your slut mouth and suck my clit so hard- and then my juicy labia-along with it- for tender pleasure-Girl fun, of being an erotic lesbian.

Katherine was nervous-but done what she had asked her to do- she gently places her hand on her clit and starts to rub it in a circular motion way-watching Black Velvet facially giving expression going wild with pleasure and melting away with every stroke that she would use to arouse her in a sexual way, of pleasure. As she was stroking her fingers on her clit-and orbiting it all around it, like a sweet tongue feather, she would get her kicks out of it, and loving it-as she knew that she was in a land that all these dirty things were fine to perform, on these lands.

Katherine starts to moan out loud with desire, of hunger, to eat Black Velvets cunt out. Gradually she spreads her legs wide open, just a bit more, so she could place her head in between her legs, and place her entire tongue in her sweet aroma cunt of hers. As Black Velvet, had spread her legs open, she begins to moan out loud and starts to cry out for more deep tongue penetration, by her. That was one of her favourite positions, she loved when Katherine would soak her tongue deep inside her wet pussy and then tenderly teasing her-deep inside of her, by moving her tongue in and out and then slowly wiggling it in her mouth, allowing her cum juices to roll in Katherine's mouth, as sweet as honey-does, and tastes.

Hungrily Katherine would enjoy it, and Black Velvet would hold her head very close to her cunt so she could place her face into her entire horny pussy, so she could taste her.

As Katherine decides to place her wet tongue deeper inside of Black Velvet Clit, and stroke it for a long time-to give her a feeling of lust desire by her- her vagina juices were running down on her tender tongue, with excitement. Slowly she moves her tongue to her vagina opening and places her fingers inside her hole, and gradually moving it, all around inside her, at the same time she had sticked her tongue inside her cunt giving it extra pleasure.

'Wow', said Katherine-bringing Black Velvet cunt lower to her face and placing her sexy legs on her bare shoulders, and getting her pussy closer to her mouth-as possible- sucking her clit hole deeply-as far as she could go, with it-which felt so good with her wet lusty tongue of hers.

"Do it again-and again," she begs her desperately. Black Velvet demands, with an urge, to get her to do what she wants.

"It feels so good, fuck me with your tongue," she demands again in a bossy voice- that would turn Katherine on, completely.

Katherine, gets so excited, listening to her demands-and placing Black Velvet on her bed- where she was all nude in display for her to see her- she spreads her legs wide open and observes her beautiful American African vaginal cunt-which was milky with drips of cum- rolling down on her legs from excitement.

Her chocolate tan cunt had a bit of creamy cum-rolling down from her hole-which she had a desire to bite into it and taste her cum.

She spreads her legs wide open, wider this time, and glance her pussy in view and then pats her cunt first, as an indication that she approves of her sexy creamy cunt, Cumming.

Her body language was clear to understand-that she wanted to eat her cunt out-so badly.

It was what she really wanted and this is what she has been waiting for-all this time-to explore her entire body with her, as one soul-together, as they wanted to be naughty.

As she touches her vagina hole- she melts away- loving her wetness of cum that she had release from her sweet innocent cunt of hers. Asking her to place her fingers, on her cunt and giving it a good rub- once she was rubbing it to- get it moisten up and produce wetness-of excitement.

Black Velvet cunt was floating out from her sweet hole cum- the lightest cum of desire, was coming out and giving a sign that she was waiting for her to get fucked.

Katherine keeps stroking her cunt hole with her tip of her tongue-giving long strokes and getting it wet to give her extra pleasure, of wants.

"Oh-my Katherine!" - More wet cum is coming out my pussy, and can- I come in your mouth-can I, please?" Replies Black Velvet to her.

"Oh-my Katherine!" As - Black Velvet-Yells out- 'You are going to make me cum again, and I am going to want you to fuck me harder with your strap on cock, toy.'

Katherine wants to taste Black Velvet pussy cum in her mouth-she begs for Black Velvet to get an organism, and release it on her erotic tongue, that was pierce.

She wants Black Velvet to release it in her mouth completely and spray her mouth with her cum flavours, of desires, that was floating out from her honey cunt, of hers.

'Cum for me, Black Velvet,' She begs her, "Cum in my mouth, let go-completely."

"I want to taste you completely- I love how your cunt aroma tastes in my mouth-keep Cumming-like a humming bird- who loves pleasure and flight for air -let me taste you-my love."

Katherine moves Black Velvet lower pelvic- closer to her mouth- allowing her to taste her a bit more in flavour, and tasting her aroma again and again, in her hungry mouth-where her pussy was glued to her tongue.

While Black Velvet was letting go with her multiple organisms-Katherine mouth was enjoying oral pleasure, and the releases of her cum-was what she wanted.

Black Velvet cunt kept shooting multiple organisms- many releases in Katherine's mouth-feeling her wetness in her tender cunt with her sweet touches of her tip tongue. Gently, she slides her fingers inside her vagina-giving her pleasure-of joy, along with her mouth, sucking.

Black Velvet bends her head back-and starts to moan again as a wolf, at the same time- she is satisfied with what she is doing to her, and surrenders.

'Oh, Yeah, that feels so good-Fuck me with that strap on cock, she demands-I want you to make me feel so good. Black Velvet demands it with a strong voice, for Katherine, to perform, the way she wants her to do so.

Katherine goes into the night drawer and pulls the strap on cock out-and place's it around her hips and buckles it on her firm waist-allowing the toy cock to hang low between her two legs, displaying that she is a man lover-in a woman, format.

Black Velvet gets excited and moans, loud and starts to stroke the toy cock in her hands for excitement play-then she saw the toy balls that were attached to the kinky strap on cock-and starts to squeeze them lightly in her hands, as she moans loudly. She loves, how big they were in size-to play with, and extremely horny, with the sight of them, being so big in size.

'Wow,' she replies, -"I love big balls they turn me on, completely-can I squeeze them a bit more, with my hands-for enjoyment?"

'Sure', Katherine replies. "You are arousing me totally turning me on-look at my nipples they are getting really hard and excited-need to be sucked on-and get them arouse, again."

Katherine asks Black Velvet to bend over to her mouth and suck her nipples for her pleasure, before she inserts her cock into her pussy hole, and please her.

Black Velvet moves forward to Katherine's breast and fondles with her breast nipples and starts to play with her breast nibs, and starts to bite on them tenderly.

She was enjoying playing with her nipples, and getting them hard for her enjoyment-play.

Katherine's nipples were arouse in Black Velvet's mouth-she twirls and bites on them hard to get them arouse and get a nipple erection from them-of excitement, to start their licks, of play.

Softly, Black Velvet orders Katherine to fuck her cunt out hard and long-sliding her in position by guiding her cock in the direction of pleasure to get fucked, by her.

"Fuck me"-She begs Katherine. "I really need it, so badly."

"I really want it so badly, I am hungry for a fuck."

As Katherine breast left Black Velvet's erotic mouth, of hers- biting them- in ease to turn her on-as she teases them by nipping and giving sucks.

Black Velvet would place both breasts together by grabbing them together and sucking them at the same time, with her mouth.

These were some of their tender games, which they love performing, when they felt very hot for each other.

Katherine obeys her dominating partner-and places her hard toy cock in her mouth first, for Black Velvet to enjoy the tender toy play-before fucking her pussy with it.

She knew that Black Velvet loved oral sex-she was like a Cobra Snake, hungry for his treat-that would enjoy swallowing the whole thing in her mouth-as she vibrates and makes these loud sounds-as she continues swallowing the Cock toy in her mouth.

Katherine, eyes would widen up-as she keeps watching her-and getting excited-as she was giving her the show of her life. Each moment her mouth was enlarging to glimpse the cock toy in her sweet mouth-as she looks up at her with her eyes-and nods if she likes what she is doing to her- Katherine nods back-giving her approval that it is giving her a hard erection-and how she is ready for her.

For a couple seconds, she allows, Black Velvet to enjoy the toy Cock in her mouth.

Black Velvet gets, wet and her pussy is aching for the toy cock to enter her wet cunt, of hers.

Oral sex would get them going-as the show of enjoyment was part of play-it had –all to do-about the sensations how naughty they were, with each other-and how they were able to seduce each other-and get really hot-for one another.

And, get really-really………hot and wild. As they begin to sweat-and have the need to get down to their needs.

As Katherine inserts the toy cock inside her cunt, and feels her nine inch cock going inside of her wet hole, she moans with enjoyment-and asks her how she likes it.

She makes a facial expression that she is enjoying it-and wants it to go all the way in her-deep vagina--- she wants the toy penis inside her cunt to feel pleasured-inside of her, completely.

Katherine sucks hard on her breast nipples-at times-giving her double pleasure and watching Black Velvet get turned on-by getting fucked by a toy harness Penis.

As she had the toy cock in her cunt-Katherine gets very excited-- watching how Black Velvet would stroke her toy balls, while getting fucked by her-was a thrill-she was like a "SheMale in One".

Black Velvet starts to moan and tells Katherine that she thinks that she is going to make her cum, again-and to be gentle with her-Katherine slowly removes the toy cock from her cunt hole and places it in her hot behind of hers -she slides it-in and out from her tender hole from behind-wetness of cum's rolling down.

Excitedly, Black Velvet moans with extra desire-reaching out her hands to embrace with the toy cock and tells Katherine that being a lesbian, is very desirable- in today's society.

Love-fucking with two women was always hot.

Black Velvet would announce to her in her ear, as she whispers in it- once they embrace with their dirty talks- of love fucking desires, and their dirty talks to each other-about their fetishes, which made them feel really erotic, and special-with each other.

Black Velvet expresses, how hot she feels for Katherine and wants her badly, as her fuck lover.

The two women, would embrace their hands together, while having a sexual encounter with each other and they would connect as fuck lovers, of being wild American, Women—who were free to experience, themselves, in the world.

As the toy cock was sliding all around in Black Velvets cunt, giving her extra pleasure- her cunt heated up and would get release by Cumming, from the overly buildup of sexual desires-which they had-together, that was held in-for so long-with desire.

Black Velvet wants to get anal penetration and turns to Katherine, and asks her—that she will turn over to her other side-from her behind and wants it from her, being a bit more dominating with her-as she demands the order, with what she wanted from her-and expected.

Katherine takes control of her in every way, and asks her to bend over a bit more, so she can place the artificial cock inside of her.

She creases her lovely butt with her hands, before she even starts to begin the penetration-kind of demand that she wanted.

Her love fuck wipe was her desire toy that she used at times, and she had enjoyed using it more than often-when she gave orders and give's demands-it was design to give some sexual sensations-to her thrills of desires, while commands were in demands at times, by her.

Katherine would enjoy looking at her lovely tiny butt-that was smooth and delightful to enter her with her cock toy, from her behind-as she would order her at times.

Black Velvet, knew that Katherine was in good shape-and enjoyed working out to keep her body in good shape-for her lovers.

Once, they reverse roles and Black Velvet-wore the harness around her waist-and the cock is hanging low, below her legs-as Black Velvet grabs it in her hands-and gives it a good Shake-ready to use it-on Katherine, she would rub her butt with her toy strap on cock-for a very long time, she would pre cum from her anal side-and scream out-mercy.

Katherine wasn't able to handle it-Black Velvet liked her rhythm very fast-to the point of never stopping.

Somehow,-Katherine would tell her to take it easy on her-as she was being a bit rough-as she was so excited-with how her butt looked.

She begins to moan-as Black Velvet makes sure to plug back in with her toy cock-as she starts talking dirty to her-asking her if she really-really-likes it the way she is moving it in her.

Circular motions at times-and then directly hitting her hard-as far as it can go-Katherine moans- as she knew that Black Velvet was nailing her hard- as deep as she could go-as she places her hands on her butt and brings her knees towards her-trying to get in a firm position—it was hot-as Katherine gets anal orgasm-from her behind-and release's her tensions.

As she firmly intense to give it harder to Katherine—to stimulate her needs-thrusting onto her butt-with her toy penis—as she gets comfortable with her position—as she goes deeper—and allow Katherine to get stimulated with her nine inch cock-inside of her.

Somehow, she moves her hips-around- and slightly elevates Katherine in a lower position-to make her feel it more. She begins to Scream- as she is receiving it.

Black Velvet thrusts harder-making it feel good for her- and starts to dirty talk to her—as it would turn her on the most.

Then she lifts Katherine in an angle position-deep penetrating her-as she gets on her hands to support herself.

Then she would gently rub her anal hole with her sweet fingers-as she pulls out from her behind---which Black Velvet had long pointy nails, which looked so erotic-in appearance-that looked like she was an encounter expert-and knew what she was doing.

She usually like painting them in silver tone colours with a touch of sparkles shades of colours that gave her nails a glamour look-- on the tip of her nails-she always had nail design on them, to give it a look that she was very erotic in her appearance, of style.

Black Velvet notice that Katherine butt was floating more than average, cum was rolling down from her behind-all the way from her inner thigh legs-which looked extremely erotic to her-to have it seen-in close-up.

Katherine—looked so sweet-as she meowed like a pussy cat-liking what was done to her. She was into exotic positions- and into taboo. She wore a black choker necklace with an icon of a black cat-looked like she belong in the night gale of life. She always would find what she wanted in her environment-as she was satisfied with Black Velvet performance-especially when she wore her high heel leopard shoes-in the bedroom.

Somehow animal prints had got them to get hungrier-as they both roar like wild leopards-in the bed room. It was all about-what would turn them on-as they had their own fantasy ideas-what was hot and extremely arousing to them-both.

As Black Velvet was looking at her behind butt floating out so much cum, from it-she thought that it looked like a river stream floating without an ending path to it-continuing floating down to release the juices that were holding within, her.

Black Velvet bends down on her butt, where the cum was rushing down from her cunt hole, this time- and gives her a quick lick to enhance her desire of keeping it going for a bit longer for satisfaction, with penetrating both sides, of her holes-to make her feel her vibration.

She taste's her clear cum, and enjoys how tasty it taste's in her sweet mouth.

Katherine's moans and enjoys what Black Velvet did-by tasting her and licking her rare anal behind-that needed to be licked by her, tongue-as she watches her-she wants to taste her own cum-and she scoops up a bit of her own cum with her fingers-as-she touches herself-and tastes herself-- her own cum.

Black Velvet was known as her Black tiger, which was very hunger for rare things-and at times would think that she was like another meat-eater animal-- hungry for her appetite dish.

Katherine continues to moan and moan out loud-while Black Velvet grabs her bare large breast and starts to twirl her large nipples nods-pulling them and giving her nipples a hard erection-while fucking her anal from behind-again and again, with her toy-Cock.

Katherine moans out loud again-holding on to the silky white sheets of their bedroom bed.

She keeps begging to get fuck hard and harder in her behind.

They had exchange positions—after a long period of fun--they notice something was missing.

They had forgot to use the whipping cream-as it was always use for fantasy role playing- as it served them with some benefits-as they added whipping cream on the artificial penis-and wondered if that was safe, to do so.

As, they heard that whipping Cream cause's an irritation in some sort of areas of skin-as it can also be dangerous to skin irritation, maybe even on toy cocks- and at times they would skip it-using other liqueur on their desire parts and getting high.

They always wanted to blame the bottle of whiskey –for their bad behaviours-due to the whiskey bottle—that caused them to go crazy, as they drank and had a merrily of life.

Printed in the United States
by Baker & Taylor Publisher Services